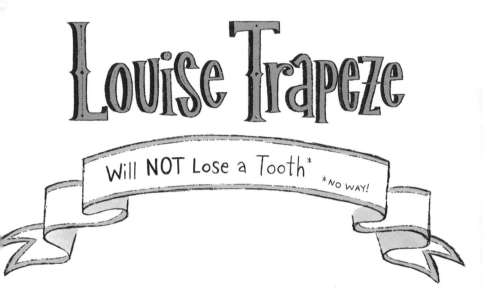

Louise Trapeze

Will NOT Lose a Tooth* *NO WAY!

FACT: You won't want
to miss a single one!!!

#1 LOUISE TRAPEZE IS TOTALLY 100% FEARLESS

#2 LOUISE TRAPEZE DID NOT LOSE
THE JUGGLING CHICKENS

#3 LOUISE TRAPEZE CAN SO SAVE THE DAY

#4 LOUISE TRAPEZE WILL NOT LOSE A TOOTH

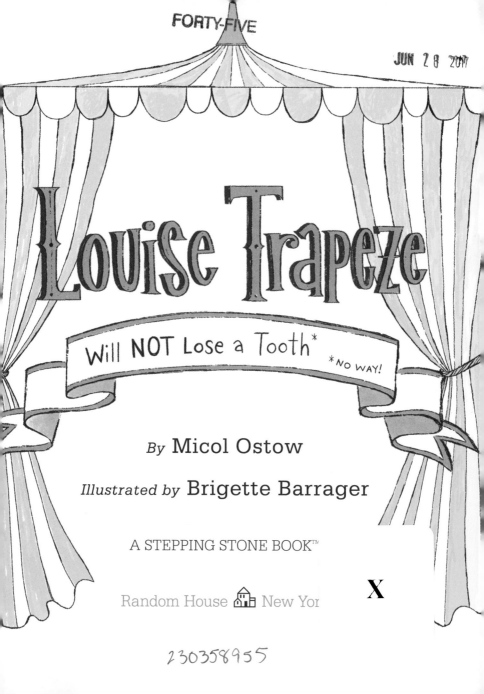

Louise Trapeze

Will NOT Lose a Tooth* *NO WAY!

By Micol Ostow

Illustrated by Brigette Barrager

A STEPPING STONE BOOK™

Random House New Yor

FOR MAZ AND NONIE

Text copyright © 2017 by Micol Ostow
Jacket art and interior illustrations copyright © 2017 by Brigette Barrager

All rights reserved. Published in the United States by Random House Children's Books, a division of Penguin Random House LLC, New York.

Random House and the colophon are registered trademarks and A Stepping Stone Book and the colophon are trademarks of Penguin Random House LLC.

Visit us on the Web!
SteppingStonesBooks.com
randomhousekids.com

Educators and librarians, for a variety of teaching tools,
visit us at RHTeachersLibrarians.com

Library of Congress Cataloging-in-Publication Data
Names: Ostow, Micol, author. | Barrager, Brigette, illustrator.
Title: Louise Trapeze will not lose a tooth / by Micol Ostow ;
illustrated by Brigette Barrager.
Description: New York : Random House, [2017] | "A Stepping Stone book." |
Summary: A young circus performer has a habit of losing things but she is
determined to keep her very loose tooth.
Identifiers: LCCN 2016002258| ISBN 978-0-553-49751-9 (hardcover) |
ISBN 978-0-553-49752-6 (lib. bdg.) | ISBN 978-0-553-49754-0 (pbk.) |
ISBN 978-0-553-49753-3 (ebook)
Subjects: | CYAC: Teeth—Fiction. | Lost and found possessions—Fiction. |
Circus—Fiction.
Classification: LCC PZ7.O8475 Lw 2017 | DDC [Fic]—dc23

MANUFACTURED IN CHINA
10 9 8 7 6 5 4 3 2 1
First Edition

This book has been officially leveled by using the
F&P Text Level Gradient™ Leveling System.

Random House Children's Books supports the
First Amendment and celebrates the right to read.

✷ CONTENTS ✷

A PERFECT MESS

"Louise! What is going on here?"

Uh-oh. I looked up from the floor of my bedroom corner. Mama had an extremely *what-on-earth?*-ish look on her face. That was never good.

In case you didn't know, I, Louise Trapeze, am one of the Easy Trapezee trapeze performers in the Sweet Potato Traveling Circus Troupe. That means I get to swing high-high-high up on the flying trapeze and do lots of big-time tricks for the audience. Can you *even*?

It also means that instead of living in a regular house, Mama, Daddy, and I travel all around the world-wide with the rest of the Sweet Potatoes in our circus trailers! This month we were in Teeny Tiny Town.

FACT: Stella and I call it Teeny Tiny Town because of the time we found the world's smallest leaf there that was shaped like a heart!

Inside our trailer, Mama, Daddy, and I all live in one long space together. So instead of a bedroom, I have my own private corner with a million-zillion secret drawers and cubbies for keeping my things tidy.

But now my things weren't tidy at all. *Actually,* they were in a huge, gigantic mess! That was why Mama was making her *what-on-earth?*-ish face at me.

The drawers beneath my bed were all half-open with ruffly costume bits and sparkly accessories spilling out everywhere. And my cubbies were empty now that all my fancy barrettes and lacy socks and things were scattered on the floor. I sat in the middle of the whole entire heap with a turquoise Mary Jane in one hand and a silver ballet slipper in the other.

I looked up at Mama and dropped the shoes. They each hit the floor with a *thunk*.

"Sorry," I said. "But I can't find my number one favoritest pair of springtime shoes! The gold polka-dot sandals with the waterproof leather straps are G-O-N-E *gone*! They disappeared right after we got to town." I frowned. "This is a *catastrophe*!"*

*CATASTROPHE = a GINORMOUS disaster that needs to be solved!! Usually by me, Louise Trapeze!

Mama's mouth twitched like she was trying not to smile. "This is definitely a catastrophe, Louise," she agreed. "In fact, I'd say this is a perfect mess. What did I tell you about keeping your things neat? No wonder you're always losing your best shoes and your favorite circus accessories. Not to mention other stuff."

"Not *always*," I said. I crossed my arms over my chest. *Always* means one hundred percent of the time. And I could think of at least three things I never, ever lost:

1. My library book of magic tricks from the Funky Town library. I returned that right smack-dab on time.

2. The teensy china horse that Daddy brought me all the way back from Paris (that's in France, a whole other *country*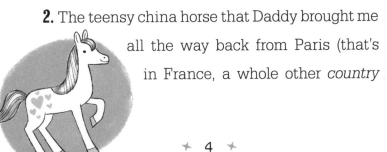

from here!). It only has the one little chip on its little horse hoof.

3. The BFF charm bracelet Stella Dee gave me when I turned six. She has an exact matching bracelet of her own! We wear them on special occasions that we plan out together beforehand. The rest of the time, I keep my brace-let on the shelf over my bed so I can see it sparkle whenever I look up.

Maybe I'm not the super-tidiest person of all times, but I hardly *ever* lose extra-special things like those sandals. This was just the strangest.

Mama raised an eyebrow. "Not *always*. But what about the baton with the spiral streamers? When was the last time you saw that?" I didn't say anything.

"And that light-up hula hoop you were using on your trampoline last month? Where did that go?"

I shrugged. *Probably* it was somewhere in our giant prop trailer, but Mama had a point. I couldn't tell her *exactly* where that hula hoop was. I glanced at my shelf, where my charm bracelet was twinkling away. I could show her that, but I didn't think it would help.

"Okay," I said. "I'll clean this all, I promise. But I can't right this second!"

Now Mama really *did* smile. "Oh?" she asked. "And why not?"

Mama was smiling because, really, she knew just what I was so excited about. I peeked at the kitty-cat clock on the wall. "Because!" I said, jumping up. "I'm late to meet Stella!"

2

EXTRAORDINARY THINGS

I needed to get to Stella lickety-split! We were going together to watch the Teeny Tiny Town Spring Carnival set up!

FAcT: There are just a few-ish things I love as much as flying on the trapeze. Cupcakes with yellow frosting is one. Another is when Mama puts bright pink streaks in my hair before extra-special circus performances.

(Don't worry—it washes out!)

And here is one other bestest-ever thing that I love: *The Teeny Tiny Town Spring Carnival!*

Every springtime, the Sweet Potato Circus makes a special visit to Teeny Tiny Town. The town puts together a giant carnival with rides, and games, and even fried cookies with sugar that you sprinkle from a shaker! We Sweet Potatoes perform special acts for the crowds. This year, I'm supposed to do my light-up hula hoop on the trampoline.

(*If* I can find it!)

A carnival *plus* a circus all smushed together into *one stupendous fun-time event!* Can you *even*?

Today everyone was setting up for the carnival, and I was ninety-six percent exploding from excitement.

Except there was one secret, four percent amount of mixed-up feelings happening to me, too.

FACT: Inside my mouth, one of my bottom teeth was a little bit hurty. Right at the part where my tooth was stuck into my gum. And also, that tooth was a little bit loose, too!

Stella had lost exactly one tooth. And Fernando Worther, Ringmaster Riley's son, had lost *seven of* his baby teeth by now. (He's nine years old.)

Only I, Louise Trapeze, had been waiting for *foreverness* for my first loose tooth. And now it was finally here! So that was one feeling I had.

But there was another feeling mixed up in my brain, too:

Actually, I was an eensy bit *afraid* about my loose tooth!

The loose tooth was a little bit hurty. So what if it hurt when it finally came out?

What if it was *bleedy*?

I do *not* like bleedy times. Not one bit. And if you're bleeding in your *mouth,* you can't even put a Band-Aid over the hurt part.

As I walked to meet Stella at the entrance to the fairgrounds, I poked my tooth with my tongue. *Yikes!* It felt even wigglier now than it did yesterday!

Well, I am the boss of my own mouth. I decided to keep all my baby teeth in there for as long as I could. And if I didn't tell anyone about my loose tooth, they couldn't say anything to change my mind.

It was going to be hard to keep my loose-tooth secret from Stella, but I had no choice!

When I found Stella at the entrance to the fairgrounds, her smile was almost bigger than her cheeks. She was so, so excited about the carnival. Behind her, Clementine waved her trunk all over the place. (That's the elephant way of being excited.)

"Sorry I'm late," I told her. "I couldn't find my shoes!" I tried to speak softly, with my mouth a little bit closed-ish, to keep the wiggly tooth a secret.

Stella nodded. She knew just which shoes I meant because of being my BFF. If she noticed my closed-ish mouth, she didn't show it.

"The gold sandals," she said. "They're so pretty." She looked down at my stripy flip-flops. "But I like those, too."

"Thanks!" I said. My tooth made a wobble, and I quickly curled my lip around it.

This time, Stella *did* make a look like she noticed what I was doing. I ignored it and made my voice as loud as I could: "Let's go see the tents getting set up!"

Off we walked. Right away, we saw lots of amazing carnival-ish things happening. To the right was the Mermaid Dunking Tank! At the dunking tank, people pay a ticket to throw a ball at a bull's-eye. If you hit the bull's-eye, the mermaid on the platform falls into the tank!

(It's a good thing she has a silvery-scaled fish tail that's perfect for water.)

The mermaid's whole entire fancy name is Katrina the Underwater Princess. When she performs, she wears a long red wig with thick-thick-thick bangs, special waterproof glitter all over her body, a seashell bathing suit top, and, of course, her mermaid tail. But right now she was just in normal clothes. Her blond hair was in a ponytail, and she looked more like a Regular Person than an Underwater Princess.

But she *also* looked very happy to see us! "Louise Trapeze and Stella Dee Saxophone! My two favorite Sweet Potatoes!" she called. She gave us a giant three-way hug. "And Clementine, too, of course," she said, patting Clem's trunk. "What are you girls performing for the carnival this year?"

"I'll probably do my light-up hula hoop on the trampoline," I said. (I just had to find it!)

"I'm going to do a human pyramid on top of Clem with my mom and dad," Stella said.

"Those sound terrific!" Katrina replied. "I hope you'll have time to take a shot at the bull's-eye."

"We for-definitely will!" I promised. We waved goodbye and walked on.

The next thing we saw was the tall-tall-tall Ferris wheel. Stella and I are *actually* old enough to go on it by ourselves now that we're seven whole years old. Even though it's a little scary way-up-high in the air, it's also super fun. Especially when you have your BFF's hand to hold.

FACT: From the top of the Ferris wheel, you can see miles and miles away. Almost to Paris, France, even!!!

Just then, Stella grabbed my elbow and squeezed hard. "Louise!" she said. "What's *that?*"

I looked to where she was pointing. There was a tent I'd never seen before. Over the tent was a black banner with swirly white writing. It said *The Great Madame Fortuna: Psychic Extraordinaire.**

*Extraordinaire = a super-grown-up way of saying the complete and total best of something

But I wasn't sure what *psychic* meant. There was only one way to find out! I grabbed Stella's hand and went running!

3

THE GREAT MADAME FORTUNA

Up close, the front of the tent was full of interesting things: a deck of extra-big cards with special drawings on them, a shiny crystal ball, and a jumble of tea mugs in jelly-bean-bright colors.

A crystal ball ... cards ... tea leaves? Suddenly, I knew where we were.

"Stella!" I exclaimed. I was too excited to worry about covering up my wobbly tooth. "I think *psychic* is the grown-up word for *fortune-teller!*"

"You are correct, my dear!"

I looked up to see an old lady coming out from behind a curtain at the side of the tent. Her hair was white, and she wore a sparkly scarf tied under her chin and a long dress with a moon-and-star pattern all over.

"Are you Madame Fortuna?" I asked.

"Correct again! The Great Madame Fortuna herself! What a smarty-pie you are!" Madame

Fortuna smiled, and I could see that some of her teeth were *gold*!

FacT: Teeth made of gold might be the fanciest ever. Probably Mama and Daddy would not let me get gold teeth once my baby teeth fell out. But what if they did?? Maybe that was one reason to be unscared about losing a tooth.

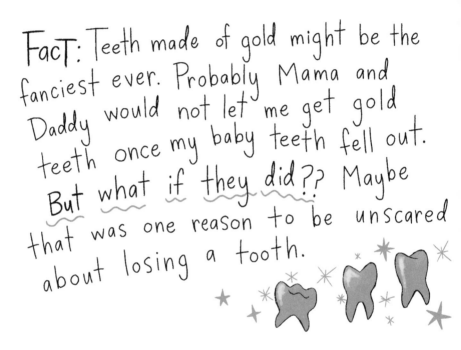

"So you can tell fortunes and predict the future?" Stella asked.

"Only if you ask nicely," Madame Fortuna said, laughing so big I could see those golden teeth again.

I looked at Stella. Stella looked at me. Neither of us had ever had our fortunes told before. It was an exciting idea but also a little bit nervous-making. Maybe Madame Fortuna would tell me that I was *finally* going to learn to do a triple backflip on the trampoline! But what if she read my future and saw something *uh-oh*-ish, like that I'd never, ever find my light-up hula hoop again?

Or—even worse—what if she predicted that my loose tooth was *for sure* going to hurt when it came out? That would be terrible news.

I wasn't sure I wanted to know the future if it was going to have some kind of *uh-oh*.

"Are you two getting your fortunes told?"

Ugh. There was Ferret-breath Fernando. For once, he wasn't wearing his stilts. But his pet ferret, Linus, was perched on his shoulder like always.

Fernando is a giant know-it-all. *Of course* he would

show up at the fortune-teller's tent just when I was feeling slightly nervous.

"We are," I told him. "Stella and I have such bright-and-shiny futures, we're definitely not scared at all." I felt a little *twinge** of pain in my tooth when I said that, but I pretended everything was completely normal and regular.

★ TWINGE = a teeny-tiny little pinch of hurty-ness, almost like a blink

Fernando raised one eyebrow at me. "Great," he said. He crossed his arms over his chest. "I'll supervise."

"We don't need supervision," Stella said.

But Fernando wasn't going anywhere. And since I'd already said I wasn't scared, now I needed to prove it.

"What fun!" Madame Fortuna said. She waved us into the tent. Stella and I gave each other a glance, but we followed Fernando in.

(Even if I *was* an eensy bit nervous, I was curious, too!)

Inside was a small, round table set up for fortune-telling. The walls of the tent were lined with shelves that held *extremely* interesting things:

magnifying glasses in all shapes and sizes, twinkly jewel-colored rocks called crystals, and dice with different squiggly symbols on them. I even saw a jar full of feathers in one corner! *Feathers!*

And then! Out from behind a curtain came a *swoosh*ing sound and a flash of fur!

Stella gasped. "It's a monkey!" she said, pointing.

It *was* a monkey! He was small and brown and wore a bow tie the same color as the moon and

stars on Madame Fortuna's dress. He swooped onto Madame Fortuna's shoulder and gave us a monkey-ish grin.

"Not just any monkey," Madame Fortuna explained. "This is Tarot. Tarot cards are special cards with pictures that I use to tell fortunes. And Tarot the Monkey is in charge of shuffling the deck for me!"

"Wow!" I said.

FacT: Tarot is one smart monkey! Even Clementine the Elephant can't shuffle cards! And she can answer yes-or-no questions — if you ask them slowly.

"Correct. He's also good at ticket taking," Madame Fortuna said. "And he can roller-skate." Tarot smiled in a proudish way at that.

She pulled three chairs around the little round table, plus one for herself. "Now," she said, settling into her seat, "which of you is first?"

Stella gave me a glance. I nodded back at her in a knowing-what-she-was-thinking way. She stepped forward, and Madame Fortuna gave her big-time laugh again.

"Wonderful!" she cried. "Let's get started!"

4

WATERY WEIRDNESS

"**F**irst things first," Madame Fortuna said. She took Stella's hand into her own. "What's your name?"

"I'm Stella Dee Saxophone," Stella said. Her voice was a little bit shy.

Madame Fortuna grinned. "Hello, Stella! This is going to be fun!" She made a thinking face. "Now that we're properly introduced, I think for you we'll try . . . the crystal ball!" She looked at Fernando and me. "Please keep quiet while I concentrate."

Fernando and I both nodded. I could tell he was as impressed as I was. A crystal ball! *Fascinating.*

Carefully, Tarot placed the crystal ball in front of Madame Fortuna. I peered at it as closely as I could, but the crystal just looked like cloudy glass to me.*

*I guess you have to be a real-live psychic to be able to see inside a crystal ball.

Only, Madame Fortuna wasn't really looking at the crystal ball. Instead, she had one hand on either side of it. Her eyes were half-closed like she was concentrating big-time.

"Hmm," she said. "I see you standing on top of your elephant friend's back."

"That's Clementine!" Stella said, excited. "My family performs with her in our act."

"No wonder I also see a grown-up man and woman on either side of you," Madame Fortuna added. "Your mother and father?"

"Is the man tall and skinny, and the woman short and skinny?" Stella asked.

"They are indeed!" Madame Fortuna agreed.

Stella gasped. "It must be them!"

Madame Fortuna pressed her hands even tighter against the crystal ball. "That image is fading, Stella," she said. "Now I see . . ." She leaned forward. "Hmm." She shook her head like she was clearing it out. "Now I see . . . water?"

Stella made a confused face. Teeny Tiny Town is not an especially watery place. There is no ocean or lake or even pond nearby. The most water that happens here is when we give Clementine a bath.

"Is it rain?" Stella asked.

"I don't think so," Madame Fortuna said. She squeezed her eyes tight-tight-tight shut. "The image I'm getting is just you, Miss Stella. You're completely soggy."

"Soggy?" Stella repeated.

"Soggy," Madame Fortuna repeated, "but happy. And there's a message, too." She took a deep breath and went on:

"Swim, Stella, swim,

With your long, silver fin."

I gasped. A rhyming fortune was *extra* special!

But Stella only wrinkled her forehead. "That doesn't make any sense," she said. "I don't *have* fins. And there's no place to swim around here."

Madame Fortuna opened her eyes and took her hands off the crystal ball. "My predictions are always guaranteed," she insisted. "I guess we'll just have to wait and see."

"We'll have to keep an eye out for watery weirdness," I said.

Stella nodded. "I guess so," she said. "But what about *your* fortune, Louise?"

My stomach went fluttery. Stella's fortune-telling went so well—with rhyming and everything!—even if we didn't know what her watery weirdness was going to be. Now I was even more nervous about maybe getting an *uh-oh* fortune myself!

Madame Fortuna really *was* a psychic extraordinaire. Her predictions were even guaranteed! So what was she going to see for *me*?

5

HERE COMES THE UH-OH!

"And now, my dear, may I have the pleasure of *your* name?" Madame Fortuna asked, turning to me.

"Louise Trapeze," I told her. "I'm one of the Easy Trapezees."

"Well, that makes perfect sense," Madame Fortuna said. "Because you have a very airy aura about you. Your aura is your energy," she explained.

My energy was very airy and trapeze-ish! That

was good news. (I think—I'm not *totally* sure what aura-energy really is. It sounds kind of like a special magic cloud floating around me.)

"Now," Madame Fortuna said, "for your fortune!"

I was holding my breath from excitement and nervousness. For a second, I even forgot to keep my lip curled close to my loose tooth. Madame Fortuna wrapped her hands around the crystal ball again. She stared off into space for a minute or two. Next to her, Tarot made a squeaky monkey sound. "Shh," she told him gently.

It got very quiet while Madame Fortuna concentrated. I poked at my tooth with my tongue again and tried to pretend I wasn't worrying. After a moment, Madame Fortuna took a deep breath.

"I see . . . you twirling around a trapeze bar?"

"Oh my goodness gracious!" I cried. "That's me doing a hip circle! I'm *superb* at hip circles!"*

*It's not bragging to say you are superb at something if it happens to be the for-definite truth.

Madame Fortuna smiled at that. But then her smile faded. "Louise, I'm getting a *strong* reading for you."

Eek! I thought. *Good strong? Or not-so-good strong?*

Madame Fortuna's mouth scrunched all up. My stomach gave an eensy flip-flop. My fortune was starting to look not-so-good. She spoke again:

"There is no cost
To what is lost."

Double eek! "Lost?" I asked.

Fact: Bad news is still bad news, even if it rhymes. And lost things are bad news!

Maybe Madame Fortuna was talking about my light-up hula hoop? That was *priceless* to me, which is a fancy way of saying it *has no cost*. The same with my gold shoes!

I felt another twinge in my mouth and remembered something else that had no cost: my tooth! Losing my first tooth would be big-time priceless.

Maybe that's what she was predicting—that I was for-definitely going to lose my tooth?

Oh no! Those mixed-up feelings came *whoosh*ing back. This was it, exactly what I'd been afraid of—an *uh-oh* fortune from the Psychic Extraordinaire!

6

YOU BET

Fernando let out a big-time *snicker.**

* Snicker = a mean, gooberish kind of laugh that Ferret-breath Fernando is especially good at

"You're going to lose something, Louise!" he said. "Hope it's not your mind!"

Our readings were over, and Stella, Fernando, and I were back outside Madame Fortuna's tent again.

Stella gave me a worried look. "Maybe it won't come true," she said.

I frowned. "But everything else Madame Fortuna said was totally and completely correct," I pointed out. "She knew about you performing on Clementine's back. And she also saw my superb hip circle in the crystal ball! So this will probably turn out true, too."

It made me feel peanut-butter-lumpish in my throat to think that, but I had to *face facts** like the ninety-eight percent fearless person that I was.

* FACE fACTS is a grown-up way of saying "deal with the truth of things even when they're uh-oh-ish."

Fernando said, "You *are* pretty great at losing things, Louise. What about the time you lost the juggling chickens while you were giving them a bath?"

Fact: Chickens *Love* bubble baths!

He was teasing, but it still made me feel bad. I stamped my foot. "That was an accident!" How was I supposed to know that chickens get very slippery in a bubble bath?

"Well, no one ever loses things on purpose," Fernando pointed out. "Anyway, I bet this is one fortune that *for sure* comes true."

Ooh, that made me the angriest. Especially since I was still a little bit afraid about losing my wobbly tooth.

Before I could stop myself, words came wave-crash-rushing out of my mouth. "Well, *I* bet you don't even know what you're talking about!" I shouted.

(I was still careful to keep my lower lip tight as ever, even when I shouted. And that is *not* easy to do!)

Fernando shrugged. "Okay, then it's a bet. I bet you're going to lose something. And soon!" He grinned and wagged his eyebrows in a joking way.

But I didn't feel very jokey about any of this! *Grr.*

Fernando held out his hand to me. "If it's a bet, we have to shake on it. That's what grown-ups do."

Double grr. Betting Fernando did not sound like the very best idea. Especially since I thought he was probably right—Madame Fortuna's prediction would totally come true.

But those wave-crashing feelings were too-too strong. "I *know* what grown-ups do!" I snapped.

Before I could stop myself, I reached out and shook Fernando's hand in a firm, grown-up way.

Fernando shook my hand right back, with all his might. "It's a bet, then."

"What does the winner even get?" Stella asked.

Fernando looked at Stella like she was totally crazy-bananas. "The winner gets to *be the winner,* duh."

As soon as we finished shaking hands, that peanut-butter-lumpish feeling swelled up in my throat again, even bigger than before. *What did I get myself into?*

Stella grabbed my hand. "Just you wait, Fernando," she said. "Louise is going to win, and you'll be sorry."

She turned to me. "Let's go, Louise. It's time for siesta, anyway."

We said goodbye, and I followed Stella back to our trailers. My feelings weren't mixed up anymore. Now they were completely and totally bad-mood feelings!

My tooth was loose. It was probably going to fall out. So that was one thing I would lose—a maybe-*hurty* thing! And who knew if I'd ever find my shoes, or my hula hoop, or any of the other things that were missing? There was no way I could win this bet.

If only I hadn't lost my *temper,* too!

7

SIESTA SECRETS

Stella was right—it was time to go back to our trailers. It was siesta* time for the Sweet Potatoes.

★A SIESTA is sort of like a nap, but fancier because of how the word is Spanish.

But I didn't think I'd be able to siesta today. My stomach was all fizzy like a shook-up soda. I was still thinking about my *uh-oh* fortune . . . and my bet with Fernando.

When I got to my trailer, I quickly cleaned up the tornado-mess I'd left behind in the morning. I was so full of energy that it took no time.

But while I was cleaning, I noticed something strange: my silver BFF charm bracelet was missing!

I was eighty-three percent sure I'd left that bracelet on the little shelf above my bed. It was there when I left to meet Stella earlier! That's where I *always* put it for safe-keeping.

(Mama says it would actually be safer to keep it in a box, instead of out on the shelf in the open. And it was looking like she might be right!)

Hmm. I flipped my pillow over to see if the bracelet had fallen off the shelf. But the bracelet wasn't there.

Suddenly, I heard a quiet-ish scuffling sound from the other side of the trailer. *What was that?*

I turned to look, but the trailer was totally and completely empty. Mama and Daddy were in town, shopping. And the rest of the Sweet Potatoes were in their own trailers, of course. I was definitely, totally alone.

So why didn't it *feel* like I was totally alone?

Louise Trapeze, you are imagining things, I decided.

Maybe I really *did* need a siesta after all. My mixed-up feelings had turned into mixed-up *thinkings*. I'd have to look for my bracelet—and everything else that was missing!—later on.

I didn't think I'd ever fall asleep, but I was wrong. One second, I was lying down on my bed, and the next minute, I was blinking my eyes open again. I wasn't feeling fizzy anymore. Now my brain was all cobweb-crowded. (Daddy says that's normal for just-waking-up times.) My mouth was even a little droolish, too!

I reached for a tissue to wipe the drool away. But when I did, I realized:

My loose tooth was wigglier than ever!

Oh no!

Fact: I was doing not-the-best job of being the boss of my own mouth. That tooth sure wanted to come out!

There was a tiny mirror sitting right on the shelf over my bed. (Next to where the bracelet was supposed to be!) I grabbed it and made the most wide-mouth face I could.

I didn't see anything different. The tooth still looked very regular-tooth-like. But when I tapped at it, it jiggled like a bowl of raspberry Jell-O.

Fact: I wasn't going to be able to hide this loose tooth for much longer...

But also:

Fact: I wasn't ready for it to come out, either!!!!!

I had no worldwide idea what I was going to do.

I was trying my hardest to figure out a solution when I heard it:

A *shout*!

And it was coming from the carnival tents!

8

THE MERMAID'S APPRENTICE

Quick-quick-quick, I jumped into my shoes and ran down to the fairgrounds to see what all the shouting was about. Right away, I found Stella standing in front of Katrina's tent. "Louise!" Stella cried when she saw me. "You heard it, too."

"Mmm-hmm," I replied. I was super curious about what was going on, but I still tried to keep my lower lip curled close in. I needed to protect my poor hurty little tooth and *also* keep anyone else from noticing its looseness—for as long as I possibly could!

"What's going on?" I asked, looking around. Just behind Stella, Katrina was standing beside her dunk tank. She looked *very,* extremely worried. "Was that you shouting, Katrina?"

My words sounded softer and more mumble-ish than ever because of all my lip curling. Stella was definitely giving me a funny look now. Katrina, too. But they didn't say anything, thank goodness gracious.

Katrina sighed. "It sure was. You see, my baby sister was supposed to join me for this year's carnival," she explained. "We were going to be the Underwater Princesses—she would be my Mermaid Apprentice! And we were going to take turns in the dunk tank so that I could keep my booth open extra late."

"That's a superb idea!" I said. Two mermaid princesses would be double the mermaidy fun!

For a minute, I was *so* excited. But when I said the word *that's,* my tongue pushed on my loose tooth. *Ouch!* And *whoops!* My eyes went wide, and I put my hand over my mouth quick-quick-quick.

Stella gave me a weensy-bit-funnier look. "Is something wrong, Louise?" she asked.

"I . . . uh . . . bit my tongue," I mumbled, keeping my face turned slightly away from everyone. "Ow."

Katrina made a sympathy face at that. But then she tilted her head at Stella and me like she was having a *eureka!* moment.

"Louise," she said, "I know you've got your special light-up hula hoop act lined up for the carnival. But maybe, Stella, you'd like to fill in for my sister as my apprentice? Work the dunk tank with me?"

"Oh!" Stella looked very surprised.

Actually, she looked surprised in maybe not the good way.

"Um, sure." She pushed a smile onto her face, but it wasn't one hundred percent real. (A BFF knows these things.*)

✳ Three BFF For-Examples of Stella's Non-Real Smiles:

1. When her grandmother gave her a brown knit scarf for Christmas, even though brown is Stella's most un-favorite color. But Stella still wanted to be polite, of course.

2. When there were only black jelly beans left at the Sweet Potatoes'

annual Halloween party. (Black jelly beans are spicy and make Stella sneeze!)

3. When she got a haircut before her sixth birthday and the haircutter made it too-too short. Stella was an *extremely* good sport about that haircut.

I would have to ask Stella about her non-real smile later, when we were alone. But in the meantime, I realized something.

"Stella!" Her name came out of my mouth like a hiss because of my lip curling. "Madame Fortuna's prediction—it came true! Remember? She said she had a vision of you and *water*! And the rhyme! It said you would *swim* with your silver *fin*!"

Madame Fortuna was a one hundred percent superb psychic, no doubt about it. Good news for Stella. But bad, badder, *baddest* news for me!

Stella blinked. For a minute, her face went for-seriously excited. "You're right, Lou!" she said. "I can't believe it!" Then she frowned. "But do you think that means that *your* prediction will come true, too? Do you think you're going to lose something?"

Not if I can help it! I thought. With my lips pressed together, I poked my tongue against my loose tooth. It was the most one hundred percent wobbly of ever by now. My heart skittered as my tooth wiggled and jiggled.

It didn't seem fair that Stella got to be a Mermaid Princess while I just got to have a hurty old loose tooth. It was time to be a grown-up, un-jealous BFF. (That would be hard work, but I, Louise Trapeze, am *actually* very mature.)

I turned to Stella and spoke as clearly as I could while still staying curled-ish.

"Why worry about that right now?" I said. "Let's get you all trained and prepared! You're going to be a *mermaid*!"

9

SINK OR SWIM

"**N**ormally, I can only keep the dunk tank open for a few hours," Katrina explained. She, Stella, and I were standing in front of her tank as she showed us exactly how it worked.

There were wooden steps at the back side of the tank's platform that led up to a small plank. The plank stretched over the opening of the tank, where all the water was. When Katrina was being the Underwater Princess, she'd sit on the plank with her mermaid's tail curled very dainty-ish. She'd smile and wave when people came up to take their turn dunking.

And *then*! The people who came to the dunk tank would give tickets in order to take a chance throwing a beanbag at a special bull's-eye

connected to the wooden plank! If they had very good aim and threw the beanbag nice and hard, it would hit the bull's-eye in just exactly the perfect-most spot. And *kaboom!* Down Katrina would go, into the tank!

When she was floating in the water, her long red wig would wave all around, and her glittery skin and silvery tail would sparkle. It was *amazing*. Katrina was probably the most magical mermaid of evertimes.

"The very longest I can usually work the tank is four hours, tops," Katrina said. "After that, the water makes my skin too pruney."*

★Pruney = shriveled, like when you're in the bathtub for too-too long and your fingertips pucker up like raisins

"But with you here, Stella, we can probably add another two whole hours onto the act! I could do two hours, then you could do one—and then we'd do that all over again. Simple!"

Katrina dashed into her tent quickly and came back with a mini mermaid costume on a hanger. "This is the outfit I had made for my sister," she said.

The outfit Katrina was holding up was so completely spectacular, my eyeballs almost popped right out of my head. It was a smaller version of Katrina's costume, right down to the seashelly top and the sequiny tail.

When I saw that extra-glittery tail, I did *not* feel adult-ish or mature.

Stella is my BFF, that's true. But also, she is almost always perfect at everything she tries. Her hair is never twisty-noodle crazy like mine. She doesn't lose important things like light-up hula hoops, the way I do. And she isn't afraid of losing her baby teeth.

Stella's fortune was a sequiny mermaid's tail. *My*

fortune was a hurty loose tooth that I was scared to tell anyone about. It was so, so not fair.

Fact: Being this un-jealous and mature was the hardest!!! I deserved a prize for it!!

MOST UN-JEALOUS AND MATURE

"Try the costume on!" I said in the best happy voice I could do. "Then we can practice your dainty sitting and your graceful falling-into-the-water."

"Exactly what I was thinking," Katrina said.

"Great minds think alike," I replied.

Stella didn't look like she was thinking alike with us, though. She peered at the costume. "It looks too small," she said.

Katrina bit her lip. "I doubt it," she said. "It's made to stretch."

Stella shrugged. "But it's so pretty," she said. "We should keep it clean and dry for the show."

"It's a special material that dries quickly," Katrina said. She was starting to sound a little confused.

I was confused, too. Why wasn't Stella eager to try on her amazing costume? "You could always try the tank just in your bathing suit," I suggested. "Like to practice."

"That's a great idea," Katrina agreed.

Stella made a not-so-sure face. "Is the water super cold?"

"It's pretty warm," Katrina said.

Stella was being so strange! "Do you want me to test it for you?" I asked. *Someone* had to!

Before Stella could answer, I scampered up the steps to the plank. I inched out over the water on my stomach as carefully as I could and dangled one arm off the plank, trying to reach the water.

Only, I must have dangled too-too far, because the next thing I knew, I was sliding off the plank— *splish-splash-splosh!*—and into the dunk tank!

Eep!

"Louise!" Katrina called. She rushed to the edge of the platform and reached for me. She tugged hard to fish me out.

Once we were back on the ground, she asked, "Are you okay?"

"I'm fine," I said. "Just drippy."

It was mostly true. But water was *splooshing* all

down from my twisty-noodle hair, along my back, and even into my shoes. And even though it was a sunny day, I was getting goose bumps from being soaking wet.

Suddenly, I felt a tingle in my nose. My head must've wanted to sneeze out all that watery-ness, because the next thing I knew I let out a gigantic *"ah-CHOO!"*

I smacked my hand over my mouth and nose for politeness. I sneezed out two more giant *ah-choo*s. And when I took my hand away, there it was:

My tooth!

My loose tooth had completely fallen out!

10

A TATTOOED MARVEL

I looked at the tooth in my hand.

I looked at Stella and Katrina.

Stella and Katrina looked at me.

I couldn't believe it! *I lost my first tooth!*

Madame Fortuna's prediction came true! I lost the bet with Fernando! And I for definitely wasn't the boss of my own mouth.

Everything had happened so fast-fast-fast, it was a complete and total surprise. I didn't have time to feel any hurty-ness. But now that it was over, I was *holy-trapeze* shocked.

And I wasn't the only one! Stella's mouth was wide open.

I didn't blame her. Keeping loose-tooth secrets is not a very BFF way to be. I felt my face go all tomato red. I didn't know what to say to her.

My brain was jumping around like popcorn. The very last thing I wanted was to explode from embarrassment in front of Stella and Katrina. There was only one thing I could think to do!

I ran!

I *zoomed* down the row of carnival tents until I got to the end. I found a half-up tent next to a tall, leafy tree. My breath was very fast-ish and my face was hot, so I stopped running and sat—

thump—crisscross-applesauce under the tree.

It wasn't until I was sitting that I noticed someone else beneath the next tree over, reading.

"Where's the fire?" that someone asked.

"What?" I didn't see a fire anywhere.

That someone laughed. "It's just an expression. I was wondering why you're in such a hurry."

I looked at him. Normally, I would be super excited to learn a fancy new expression like *where's the fire?* But right now, I was distracted.

Because this man was totally and completely *one hundred percent covered in tattoos*!

Of course, I've seen tattoos before. Cady the Bearded Lady has bunches and bunches of tattoos on her arms and legs. And Stella and I love doing glitter tattoos at our sleepover parties. (Ours are the wash-off kind.) But I never in my whole lifelong time saw *anyone* with as many tattoos as this man. His body was more tattoo than regular skin!

The man noticed my wide-open mouth. "I'm Frankie the Tattooed Marvel. This is my first year with the carnival." He folded over a corner in his book to save his place. Then he reached out and shook my hand like I was an actual grown-up.

"I'm Louise Trapeze," I told him. "I'm with the Sweet Potato Circus. My family's the Easy Trapezees."

"Trapeze! That's my favorite of all the circus acts," he said, smiling.

"Mine, too!" I said.

Fact: People who love the trapeze are the _best_ kind of people, I think. Because we can ≡*FLY*≡ in our special trapeze way!

"So tell me, Louise: why do you look so down?" Frankie asked.

I bit my lip. I was still holding my just-fell-out tooth tight-tight-tight in one fist. I didn't want to tell him about today being not actually very great. But he was being so nice. And it sounded like he really wanted to know what was bothering me.

"A lot of things went wrong today," I said softly. "First, I lost my favorite shoes. And Mama reminded me that I lose things a *lot*. Including my light-up hula hoop that I'm supposed to use in my special carnival act. And then Madame Fortuna read my future and my best friend Stella's. She predicted that Stella would have water in her future—and then Stella was picked to be the Mermaid Apprentice!" I swallowed, remembering how jealous that made me feel.

"Well, what did she predict for you?" Frankie asked.

I made a grumpy face. "She predicted I would *lose something else!*"

"Hmm," Frankie said. "I'd be upset with a fortune like that, too."

"Really?" I asked in my most hopeful voice. It was

nice to know that Frankie didn't think I was being babyish.

"Oh, definitely," he said. "And I'm *totally* forgetful! So I know just how you feel. In fact"—he leaned in—"the very first tattoo I ever got was this one." He held out his arm to me. Right by the bendy part of his inside elbow was a small red playing card. It was the ace of hearts.

"Ace was the name of my first puppy ever. We were best friends. And when he died, I got this tattoo so I'd always remember him. Then it turned out I *loved* tattoos. So I started getting them in honor of lots of different things I wanted to remember or celebrate."

"And now you have more tattoos than regular skin!" I said.

He laughed. "Yeah, that just kind of happened. One

day I woke up and I was Frankie the Tattooed Marvel. And the rest is history."

"We learn history in our special circus classroom," I told him. "Like about countries being discovered, or things being invented, or the presidents."

Frankie laughed again. "I'll bet you do," he said. "But *the rest is history* is actually another expression, like *where's the fire?*"

I was liking Frankie more and more. He knew so many grown-up expressions, and he had SO many tattoos. Plus, he understood what it was like to lose things.

"So you lost your shoes, and you got a not-great fortune reading. What else?" Frankie asked.

Slowly, I opened my fist. "Madame Fortuna was right about my fortune. I *did* lose something: my tooth!"

Frankie leaned over and peered at the tooth in my

hand. "Whoa! That's pretty neat," he said. "Losing a tooth is a big deal. Aren't you excited?"

"I sort of am," I said. "Except also, I was scared that it would hurt when it fell out. So I kept my loose tooth a secret from my best friend, Stella. Now she's probably mad at me."

"Oh, I doubt that," Frankie said. He pointed just over my shoulder.

When I turned to see where he was pointing, there was Stella!

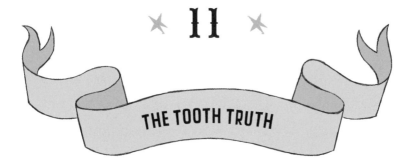

THE TOOTH TRUTH

Stella was standing right beside Katrina. She looked confused and maybe a little bit sad—but she didn't look angry.

"Louise!" she said. "Why did you run away?"

I sighed. It was truth time.

"I was embarrassed for not telling you about my loose tooth," I told her. "And I didn't want to tell you because I was scared my tooth would hurt when it fell out. That's the whole, real story."

Stella looked at me. "Louise, you know BFFs don't have to keep secrets from each other."

I nodded. "I know. But I still make mistakes sometimes."

FACT: *EVERYONE* makes mistakes
sometimes.
But sometimes it's
hard to remember that.

"I knew she'd understand," Frankie said to me. He turned to Stella. "I'm Frankie," he said, waving.

"Frankie is a Tattooed Marvel," I explained.

"Wow," Stella said. For a second, her eyes went ginormous from seeing all his jillions of tattoos. But then she snapped out of it.

Stella looked back at me again. Her face went shy-ish. "Sometimes I make mistakes, too," she admitted.

"What do you mean?" I asked.

It was Stella's turn to go tomato red. "I know you could tell I was be-ing super weird at the dunk tank."

"You *were* acting strange," I agreed.

"*My* whole, real story is: I'm afraid of being dunked in the mer-maid tank!" Stella said. She made very nervous eyebrows at the idea of it.

"But you know how to swim," I said. "I don't understand."

"Swimming in the ocean is different than fall-ing into a tank out of nowhere," she replied. "What if it feels like the bad kind of surprise—like a roller coaster loop? What if water gets *up my nose*?"

"I never thought about that," I said. "I was just focused on the fancy costume."

"It *is* a nice costume," Stella agreed. "But I may be too much of a scaredy-cat to wear it."

"No way," I told her. I stood up. "I was scared to tell you about my tooth. But when it came out, it ended up not being scary at all. I'm for certain we can find a brave solution to your problem, too."

Stella smiled. "I like that plan."

I liked that plan, too. It was nice to remember that Stella had her own Scaredness Things, just like me. And *actually*, we were excellent at helping each other out when we were feeling afraid. My jealous feelings from before were ice-cream-melting away.

"Also," I said, "we need to find my light-up hula

hoop. That way we'll *both* have extra-special acts to perform at the carnival."

"Maybe you could return this little guy to his owner while you're at it," Katrina said. She pointed behind the tree where Frankie was sitting.

I peeked at where she was pointing. Waving out from behind the tree was a skinny patch of fur. It flicked in the sunlight.

That fur patch looked familiar. I moved closer. "Tarot?" I asked.

Slowly, the tail turned around. Bit by furry bit, a small brown monkey made his way out from behind the leafy tree. It *was* Tarot!

And around his furry monkey neck was my BFF charm bracelet!

"Tarot!" I cried. "Were *you* what I heard in my trailer during siesta?"

My bracelet twinkled in the sun as Tarot nodded his little monkey head like craziness. Also, he had cotton candy stuck underneath his chin.

FACT: Monkeys LOVE cotton candy!

"You're a very messy monkey," I said. I moved closer to him to brush his chin clean.

Close up, I could see something else funny.

Not only was Tarot wearing my charm bracelet, but he had something else of mine in his paws! It was one of my hair clips—the light green one with darker ribbons that dangled down. That clip had been missing since we first came to Teeny Tiny Town. *Just like my gold sandals I was trying to find this morning!*

"Tarot?" I gasped. "Does this mean what I think it means?"

12

MONKEY BUSINESS

Creep-creep-creep went the thoughts in my brain:
Sometimes I lose things, yes (like those slippery chickens!). But I'd been losing *way* more things than usual since we got to town.

I looked Tarot right in his big brown eyes. "*You* lost my stuff! Well, not lost, actually. You've been following me and taking things!"

Tarot gave a small, monkey-ish *I'm sorry* squeak. It was hard to blame him. Of course a roller-skating

monkey would want to wear a sparkly charm bracelet for a necklace.

(Tarot had excellent taste!)

"It's okay," I said in my most gentle voice. "I'm not mad. But I'm going to need everything back. Let's go talk to your owner about this."

Tarot scampered back to Madame Fortuna's tent. I followed, with Katrina and Stella right on my heels. The tent was empty when we got there, but he quickly monkey-walked over to one corner. He stopped by a pile of cozy-looking blankets covered in monkey fur and made proud *eeh-aah-ooh* monkey squeaks at me.

I peered into the pile. Sure enough, there were more barrettes scattered around and a pair of my squishiest socks, too.* And shiniest of all—a gold strap was peeking out of the pile! *My sandals!* Now I knew without a doubt that Tarot had been following me and taking my things.

✳ It turns out even monkeys like to keep their paws warm and cozy!

"I guess it's true what they say," I told him. *"Monkey see, monkey do."*

Tarot nodded. *"Eeh-aah-ooh!"* he said.

"You're pretty cute," I told Tarot. "Even though you actually made a really big mess for me. Let's go tell Mama and Daddy that we know where my shoes are!"

"Not just your shoes, Louise," Stella said. She peeked behind a big box and pulled out something large and round. That large, round thing flicked on and off like a disco ball.

"My light-up hula hoop!" I shouted. Tarot had my hula hoop all along, too! "Now I can do my special act for the carnival."

As I was talking, I felt a little twinge of pain in my mouth again, where my loose tooth had fallen out. But I wasn't scared anymore. Everything was right-side-up-happy for me again.

I smiled wide and poked my tongue near the tooth hole. I was curious—and also super proud. The tooth hole felt empty and *very* mature.

"Hey—you finally lost a tooth, Louise!"

It was Fernando! He was back on his stilts, smirking down at me. "It's about time." He laughed. "And you know what?"

I rolled my eyes at him. "What?"

"This means you lost our bet for real." He snickered. "So, you lost *two* things today."

But this time, his mean teasing didn't bother me! Instead, I just gave a shrug. My fingers closed around my precious, priceless tooth in my pocket.

It turned out some things were worth losing!

(And *some* things were never really lost at all!)

"So what?" I said. "*Actually,* I lost lots of things. Not just the bet. But also my favorite shoes, the light-up hula hoop, and all the stuff Tarot got his tiny monkey paws on!" I pointed at the pile.

"But here it is. And anyway, I'm not the only one. Look at that blue bandanna—isn't that yours? The one you give to Linus to wear when he's feeling fancy?"

Fact: Blue is totally Linus's color. It brings out the grayishness of his fur.

Fernando looked embarrassed. "I guess. I haven't seen that in a few days," he admitted.

"Everyone loses things sometimes," I went on. "Even Frankie the Tattooed Marvel started his tattooing so that he'd remember important stuff. And now he's a grown-up with an amazing job at a carnival and everything!"

Stella and I laughed like craziness. Even Tarot gave his own monkeyish *eeh-aah-ooh.*

"I make lots of mistakes," I told Fernando. "Everyone does. But I have lots of superb *eureka!* ideas, too."

I turned to Stella. "Like as a for-instance, when I saw that barrette with the ribbons, it made me think of something else we could put ribbons on: nose plugs!"

Stella nodded. "For when I work at the dunk tank! So water won't go up my nose if I get dunked!"

"Excellent idea, Louise," Katrina said. "I can find a pair of nose plugs in Stella's size, no problem. We can decorate them so they look like a part of your costume."

Stella and I grabbed hands and squeezed. I poked my tongue at my empty tooth hole again. My heart went all squeezy (in a good way).

I didn't get everything right every day. Not hardly! But I was trying my best. Sometimes losing things was *actually* okay.

And there was one thing I'd never, *ever* lose:

My BFF, Stella!

About the Author

MICOL OSTOW is a notorious loser of things, including (but not limited to) hair ties, running socks, and fancy pens with sparkly ink. She lives and works in Brooklyn, New York, with her husband, her two daughters, and a very forgetful French bulldog. Micol is the author of numerous acclaimed books for young adults and children, but Louise Trapeze is her first chapter book series. Learn more about Micol and Louise at micolostow.com.

About the Illustrator

BRIGETTE BARRAGER is an artist, illustrator, designer, and writer of children's books. She recently illustrated the *New York Times* bestseller *Uni the Unicorn* by Amy Krouse Rosenthal. She resides in Los Angeles with her handsome husband, cute doggy, and terrible cat. Visit Brigette at brigetteb.com.

New friends. New adventures.
Find a new series...just for you!

BALLPARK Mysteries

THE FENWAY FOUL-UP

FOR THE SPORTS FAN

THE DINO FILES

A Mysterious Egg

FOR THE ADVENTURER

LOUISE TRAPEZE

Louise Trapeze IS TOTALLY 100% FEARLESS

FOR THE SUPERSTAR

PIPER GREEN

PIPER GREEN and the FAIRY TREE

FOR THE DREAMER

PUPPY PIRATES

Stowaway!

FOR THE ANIMAL LOVER

TOTALLY TRUE adventures!

APOLLO 13

FOR THE EXPLORER

RandomHouseKids.com